Bunny and Bee's
Playful Day

Sam Williams

TED SMART

For Pat, Panda, Moo, Bert and Mizzy

Also available:

Bunny and Bee's Noisy Night

ORCHARD BOOKS
96 Leonard Street, London EC2A 4XD
Orchard Books Australia
32/45-51 Huntley Street, Alexandria, NSW 2015
This edition produced for The Book People Ltd
Hall Wood Avenue, Haydock, St Helens WA11 9UL
ISBN 1 84362 387 0
First published in Great Britain in 2003
Text and illustrations © Sam Williams 2003
The right of Sam Williams to be identified as the author
and illustrator of this work has been asserted by him in
accordance with the Copyright, Designs and Patents Act, 1988.
A CIP catalogue record for this book is available from the British Library.
1 3 5 7 9 10 8 6 4 2
Printed in Singapore

Here is a house.

A house in a tree.

The house is the home
of Bunny and Bee.

Bunny   Bee

Each morning they wake
and have big, big hugs.

Then drink milk and honey
from their favourite mugs.

Bunny's mug   Bee's mug

They make their beds
and have porridge to eat.

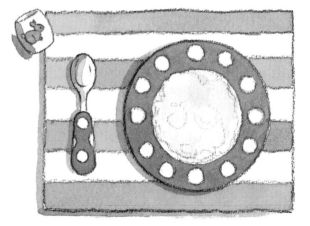

Then they tidy their kitchen,
and put boots on their feet.

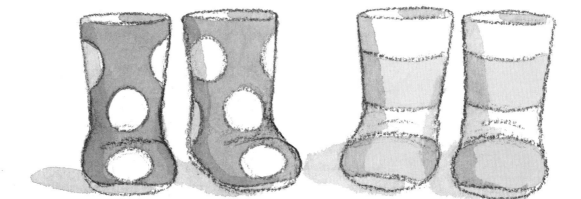

Bunny and Bee go out to play,
whatever the weather,
every day.

On sunny days they
swing in the trees.

On windy days they
chase the leaves.

On rainy days they
splash in puddles.

On cold, cold days they
have lots of cuddles.

Bunny and Bee,
like me and you,

play hide-and-seek
and peekaboo!

Bunny counts
1 2 3,
"Here I come!"
Calls Bunny to Bee.

They sing and dance
and play all day,

until the sunshine
fades away.

Then home they go
to their house in the tree.

It's bedtime now
for Bunny and Bee.

Goodnight
Bunny.
Goodnight
Bee.